A Japanese Tale

by Tim Myers

by R. G. Roth

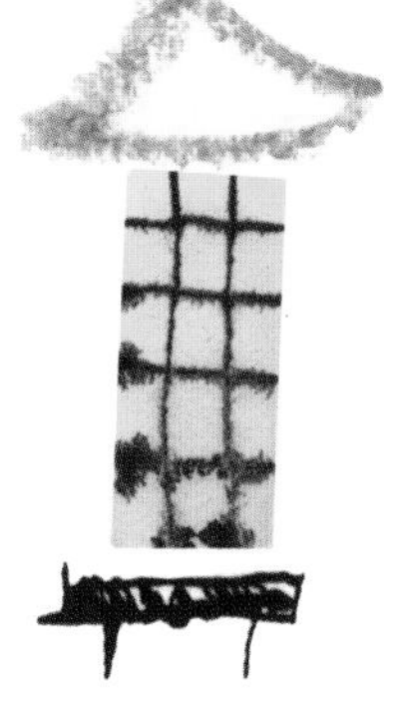

Marshall Cavendish • New York

As a classroom teacher I often had my students tell stories. One day I noticed some photocopies in the trash and, scrounger that I am, fished them out. One was of this story. But no source information was included on those wrinkled, toner-smudged pages, and only later did I track down the book they came from: Pearl Buck's 1965 *Fairy Tales of the Orient*. It turns out she based her version on A.B. Mitford's nineteenth-century *Tales of Old Japan*, which he based on stories from a Japanese pamphlet that appeared as early as 1688. I spent weeks combing numerous translated indices of Japanese folktales but still couldn't find the original.

At that point I was fortunate to have the generous help and expertise of Fran Stallings, one of our major storytellers. Fran often tours with Hiroko Fujita, a traditional Japanese storyteller from Fukushima Prefecture—and when she contacted Fujita-san in Japan, she learned of an old folktale about a tanuki who changed himself into a human to smelt gold for a priest, then died. This is a common form of Japanese folktale, an "ongaeshi" or "debt of gratitude" story, based on a social principle that, in Fran's words, "is taken very seriously in Japan." I can't thank Fran and Fujita-san enough for their invaluable help.

Stories are always changing. My ending for *Tanuki's Gift* isn't a radical departure from the Buck and Mitford versions, and I added nothing that wasn't already implicit in the story. But I was dissatisfied with their versions' predictable moral and lack of completion, which seemed to me to twist the plot unnaturally. The version in which the tanuki dies after discharging his debt may be more "Japanese," and is similar in its way to the national mythic intensity of "The Forty-Seven Ronin." But that wasn't the way the story first came to me, and it wasn't part of my shaping—and since the death occurs after the debt is repaid, I don't see it as essential. For similar thematic reasons, I kept other elements from the Buck/Mitford versions—the use of the word "priest," for example, and the reference to the traditional "Western Paradise" of the Amida sect of Buddhism, Japan's largest. Many Buddhists believe in this paradise or "Pure Lane" located, as it was said, "millions and billions of leagues in the West," where the faithful will reside in bliss after death.

Some may consider that any such shaping is a mistake, even an outright betrayal of the folk tradition. I can't agree— though I know how often folktales are crassly or ignorantly manipulated and drained of their vigor. But storytelling is a living art, and storytellers have always shaped tales. How else could great stories come to be?

In 1947, the great Japanese folklorist Kunio Yanagita recognized this implicitly when, writing about a tale called "Urikohime," he compared various versions and praised one for being "better and more beautifully arranged." Folklorists should seek superior versions of folktales, he said, as a "means for folktales to become more than a subject for scholarly research. They would become once more national treasures."

My profound admiration for folk tradition expresses itself both in a desire to preserve those traditions—and to further them. So I've carefully and humbly added my own bit of polish to an already venerable and esteemed little vessel.

—*Tim Myers*

The mixed media includes gouche, watercolor, oil pastel and ink painted on D'Arches 140 lb cold and hot press papers.

Library of Congress Cataloging-in-Publication Data
Myers, Tim (Tim Brian)
Tanuki's gift : Japanese tale retold by Tim Myers; illustrated by Robert Roth.
p. cm.
Summary: One winter, a priest takes in a furry tanuki and the two become friends,but when the tanuki tries to repay the priest, they both learn a lesson.
ISBN 0-7614-5101-3
[1. Folklore—Japan.] I. Roth, Robert, 1965-ill. II. Title.
PZ8.1.M984 Tan 2003 398.2'0952—dc21 2002009595

Marshall Cavendish, 99 White Plains Road
Tarrytown, NY 10591
www.marshallcavendish.com

Printed in China

First edition
2 4 6 5 3 1

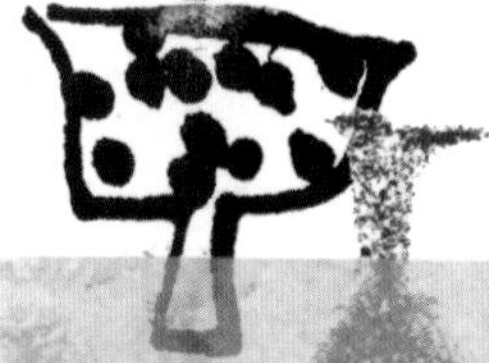

To my mom and dad and my uncle Rawl,
who gave me the love that made me who I am

—T.M.

For Cheryl, Cassidy and Grace

—R.R.

P.S. And to the memory of Buster, our very own little "tanuki". He never left us gold, but he did regard himself as the "Golden Prince of Cocker Spaniels."

Long ago, at Namekata in Hitachi, an old priest lived alone in a little hut and spent all his time praying to Buddha.

Morning and night he chanted, hoping to enter the Western Paradise when he died.

The poor people brought him food and clothes and patched his walls and roof every summer. Because they looked after him, he didn't have to think about the things of this world.

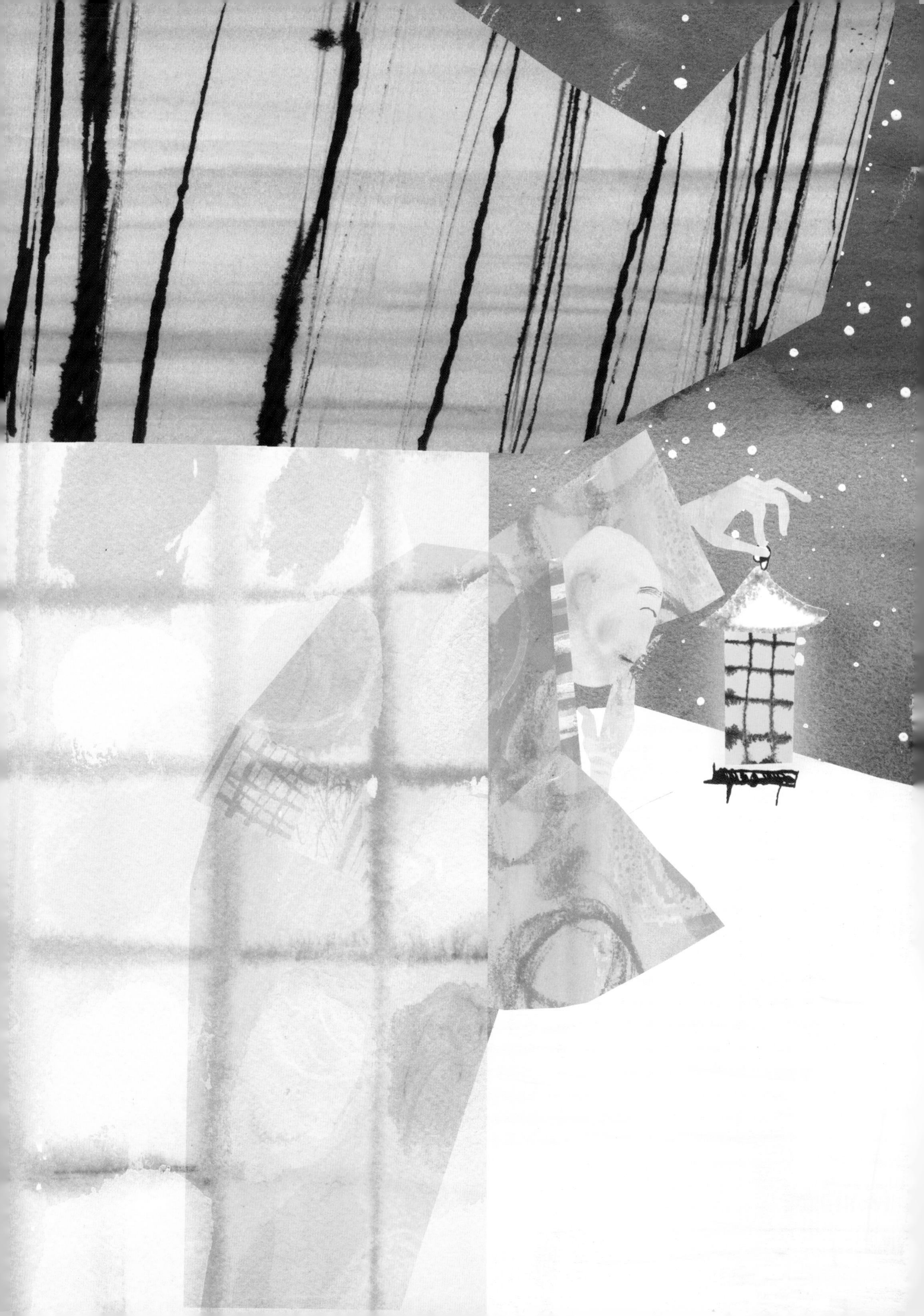

One freezing winter night, when winds came howling out of the mountains, he heard a little voice calling from outside, "Holy One! Holy One!"

When he opened the door he saw a tanuki—a raccoon-dog—standing in the snow, nearly frozen to death.

Everyone was afraid of the furry little animals, for their powerful magic and trickery were well known. But the priest saw that the creature was suffering from the bitter cold. "What is it, little one?" he asked kindly.

"I'm an orphan, Holy One," the young tanuki said, "with no family to care for me. Can I warm myself by your fire?"

"Of course," the priest replied, and the tanuki scurried in.

Soon the door was shut tight, and the hut was warm again. The priest went back to chanting and ringing his bell before the statue of Buddha.

From that time on, the tanuki came every night.

Often it would bring firewood or little gifts for the priest—shiny rocks, odd branches, and the like—and in time the priest became quite fond of it. The tanuki would laugh and dance for the old man, and tell him stories, and the priest, in spite of himself, would watch and smile. When summer came, the tanuki would stop coming—and the priest would find himself looking forward to winter, when the little creature always returned.

This went on for ten years.

Then one day the tanuki said, "Holiness, you have been so good to me, I could never fully repay you. If you hadn't taken me in, I surely would have died. So I want to do something for you. Is there anything you want?"

"You forget that I'm a priest, little one," the old man said. "There's nothing at all in the world that I want."

"Please, Holy One!" the tanuki begged. "There must be something I can do to show my thanks!"

At last the priest admitted there was one worldly thing he wanted. "It's not so important," he said, "but since you insist, if I had three riyo of gold, I could pay for prayers to be said for me so I might enter Paradise after my death."

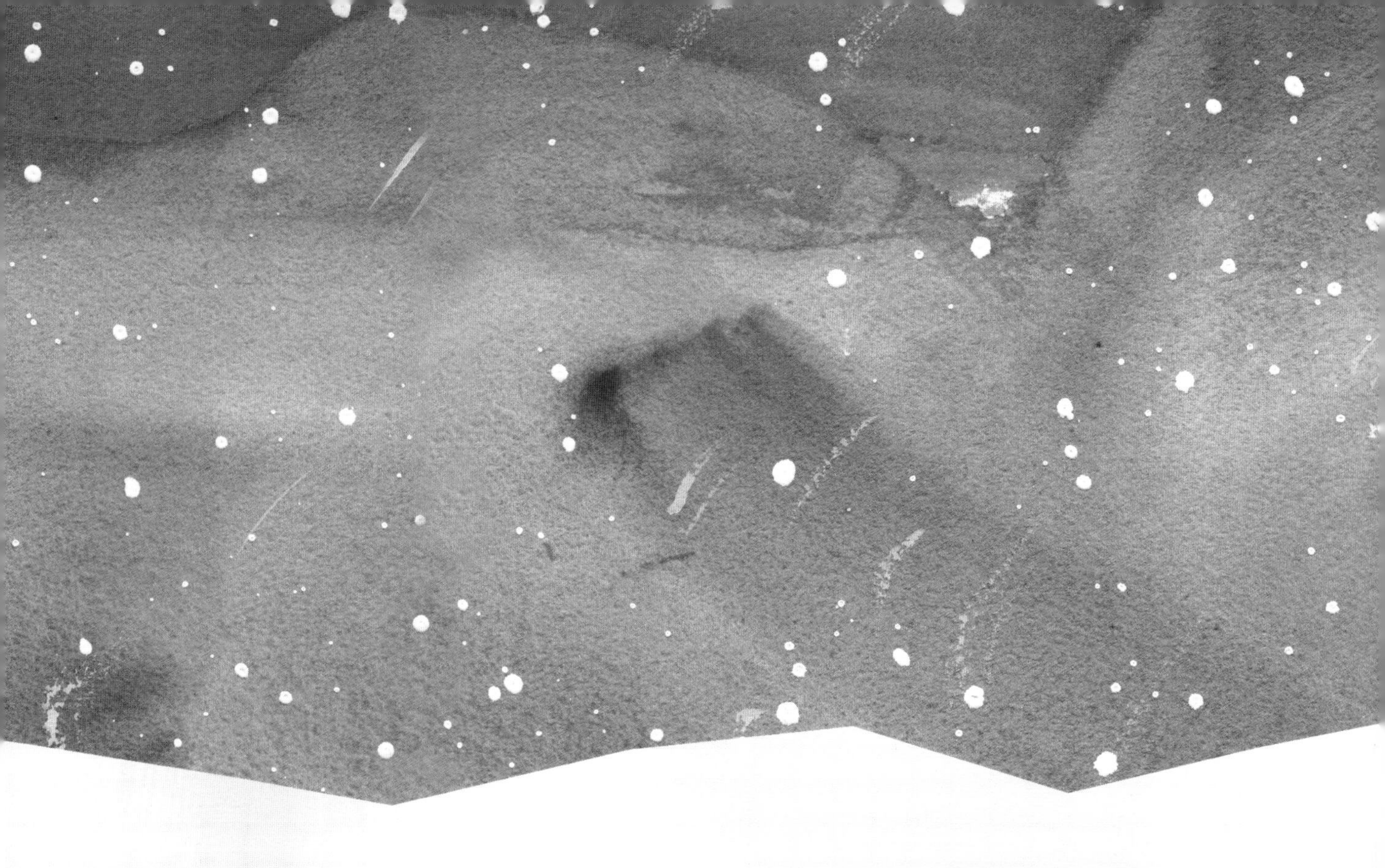

The tanuki didn't come the next night, or for many nights after. All through the winter the priest kept watch, opening his door again and again to see if the tanuki was outside. At last he decided the little creature would never return.

"Perhaps he feels ashamed because he has no money," the priest grieved, "or has been killed trying to steal it! Oh, why was I so foolish as to tell him my desire?" All winter and summer the priest suffered as he worried about the tanuki.

Winter came again. One cold night he suddenly heard a little voice outside his door. “Holy One, Holy One!” The priest’s old heart beat fast with joy.

“Where have you been for so long?” the priest asked, once the tanuki was seated again by the fire.

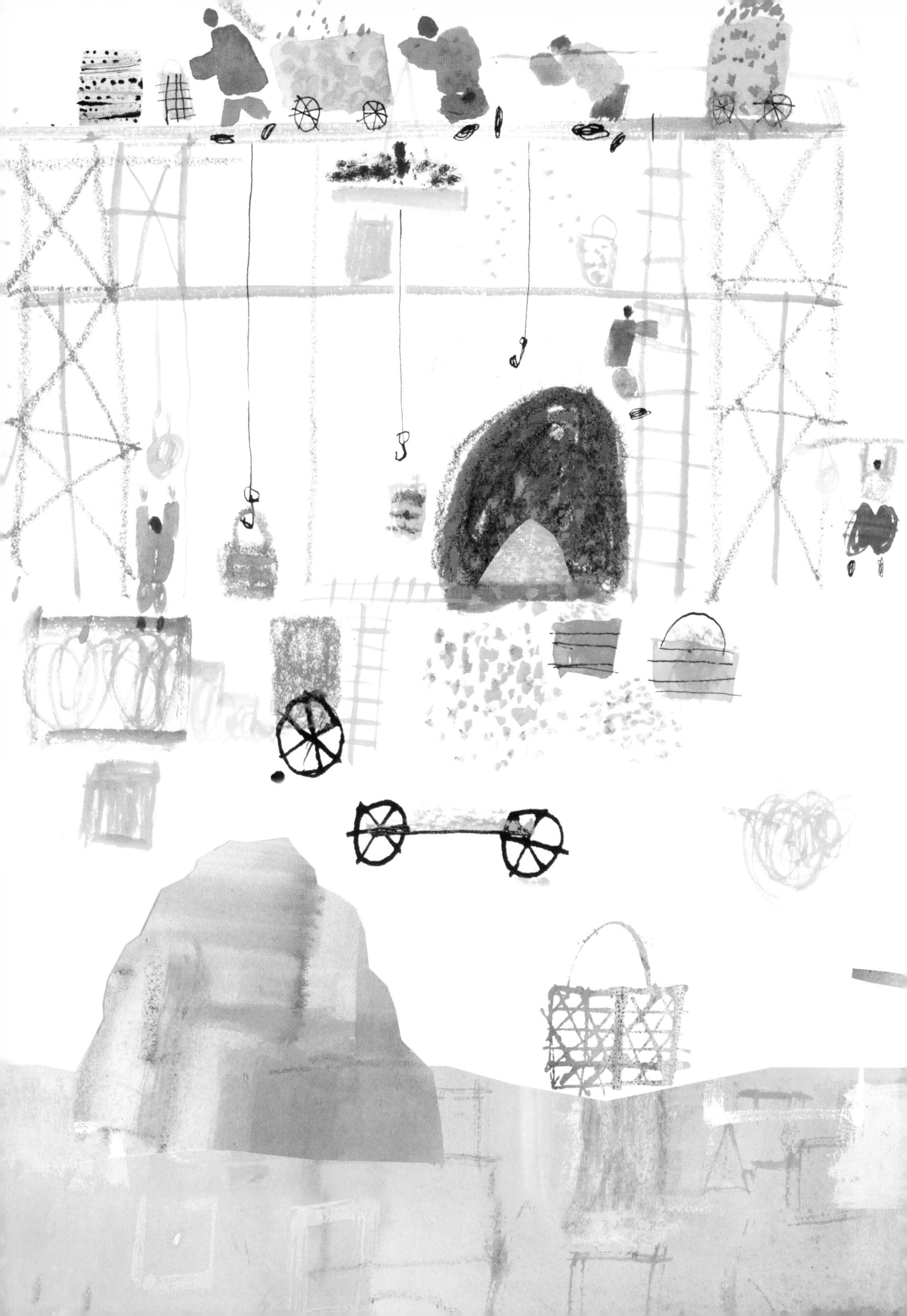

"Forgive me, Holy One," the tanuki said. "I could easily have stolen the gold—but I knew you wouldn't like that. So I went to Sado, the island where the gold mines are. And I gathered the ore the miners tossed aside, and I built an oven and smelted it.

Look! These are for you!" It held out three gleaming gold coins.

The old priest felt his eyes fill with tears for the first time in many years. "Oh, little one! I was wrong to ask for the gold!"

The tanuki jumped up, its face full of pain. "Holy One! I didn't want this to hurt you!"

The priest went to the tanuki and put his hands on its shaggy little shoulders.

"You have not hurt me. These are tears of joy! While you were gone, I learned something. I was wrong to ask for the gold, since that is not what I really wanted. And now I can give this gold to the temple, because you have already granted me my desire."

The tanuki looked surprised. "But if you don't want the gold—what have I given you?"

The priest sat down, ran his hand over his shaven head, and smiled.

"You came back," he said. "So now I have again the gift of your friendship—which is what I wanted all along."

From that day on, the priest and the tanuki were always together.